River's Trail Home

A Glimpse Into The Old West

WRITTEN BY Teresa Langley

EDITED BY Wyatt Henson

River's Trail Home
Copyright © 2024 by Teresa Langley

All rights reserved. This book or any portion thereof may not be reproduced or used in any manner whatsoever without the express written permission of the publisher except for the use of brief quotation in a book review.

ISBN: 978-1-965951-06-4 (sc)
ISBN: 978-1-965951-08-8 (hc)
ISBN: 978-1-965951-07-1 (ebk)

Seraphim Global Media LLC
155 Willowbrook Blvd Ste 110
Wayne, NJ 07470
848 800 6538
info@seraphimgml.com

River's Trail Home

A Glimpse Into The Old West

Thanks, and Acknowledgement

To my editor Wyatt Henson for his encouragement and support.
Thank you for your assistance and all your hard work.

CONTENTS

Chapter 1   Unsettling Storms 1

Chapter 2   New Beginnings...5

Chapter 3   The Lost River...8

Chapter 4   Unexpected Surprises 20

Chapter 5   Merging Families......................................30

Chapter 6   Resurfacing The Past 37

Chapter 7   Embracing Changes 50

Chapter 8   Finally Home 66

CHAPTER 1

UNSETTLING STORMS

The Morgan family's covered wagon had crossed the Mississippi River that morning on a ferry barge. Neal's mom waited on the west side as he, his brother Kenny, and Pa went back to the east side to bring the horses and cattle across. The trading post, with the docks, had an amazing view. At only ten years old, each day had been an adventure for Neal. He had grown up in Kentucky and never had been west of the big Mississippi. His Pa had found land for them in the state of Missouri's northern regions.

After a successful crossing, they headed north alongside the mighty river. Neal's Pa set up camp that evening and the four of them had a meal, then talked of the homestead they would have. Before they slept, Pa would ensure everything was ready for the morning.

Sometime after midnight Pa shook Neal and Kenny awake.

"Boys, get up." He had a very stern tone to his voice. "We have a storm coming in, I'm hitching up the team. You boys go get into the saddles, then push the herd west and head north. Get moving."

Lightning flashed, and the thunder rolled in loudly. Kenny and Neal started getting the cattle going. Kenny, three years older than Neal was also reassuring his younger brother that he was doing a good job while trying to comfort him. Kenny could see the fear in Neal's eyes each time the lightning broke through the sky with its thunderous bellows.

Kenny pulled his horse to a stop and Neal did the same.

"What is that loud noise, Kenny?" Neal spoke with worry in his voice as the rapid river rumbled, making it hard to hear each other.

"It's the river" Kenny yelled through the cacophonous roaring of the rapidly flowing river. Lightning streaked across the sky, fear filling in Neal's eyes. "Let's go, Neal! As fast as you can!" and with that Kenny took off.

Neal turned his horse to follow his brother and simply let the animal have his head. In a matter of minutes, Neal could feel something off about his horse. The horse went down and tumbled into the current. All Neal could hear as he screamed for his brother was the water's roaring start to muffle, and then grow louder as the waters swallowed him and tossed him around. He could feel the debris in the current as he got battered by brush, and trees, and being pulled under the water he had no bearings of where he was. Neal struggled to keep his head above the water, getting gasps of air between everything happening. Lightning flashed above him, as the rain's torrential downpour gave no mercy. With one of the lightning streaks lighting the area briefly, he saw that he was heading toward a very large tree up ahead. As he approached the tree and the lightning once more illuminated the sky, he saw a branch within his reach and he grasped at it with desperation and hope of escaping the river. Firmly he held onto the branch. With the current rolling underneath him, he hangs from the branch with his arms feeling like they are about to be torn off. As he felt his legs being grasped by the current, he clung to the branch. He mustered his efforts into raising his leg over the supportive tree limb. Barely managing to pull it off he starts scooting across the branch onto safer grounds. Gasping and gulping for air, he was fighting off his tears from nearly drowning. He thought his heart was going to burst out of his chest. His face leaned into the rough bark of the tree as he could see the water slowly start to rise, Neal backed up quickly looking around into the darkness surrounding him.

Moving a bit farther from the river and nesting himself into a wedge of a tree, he cried himself to sleep as the raging storm continued. The rain seemed to last forever as he was falling asleep but nonetheless, it passed him to the north as he slept. Awaking sometime in the dark morning hours, he noticed the rain had passed. The boy drifted off to sleep again, cold, wet, and alone in this dark little nook. When he awoke for the second time, he could see the dim light of the sun peering through some rather low-hanging clouds.

Suddenly he heard a whining sound. Neal looked around in confusion and started blinking his eyes to focus. He heard the sound again. Looking downward to the base of the tree his eyes met the source of the sound. It was a small puppy, clinging to a lower limb just beneath him. Leaning down he reached and grabbed it. The puppy wagged its tail.

"It looks like it'll be just the two of us." He spoke to the shivering pup. "Pa and Kenny will come and find us, boy…" He told the pup. "We just need to sit tight." Neal looked around, as far as his eyes could see, there was nothing but just the river. The water was still raging on but had only lowered by a few inches.

"We've got to be brave buddy." He spoke to the puppy in a loving, comforting way, as he let his tears start once more.

By nightfall, Neal was hungry and worried the water had only receded a few inches from what he noticed earlier. His legs straddling the big limb, the puppy laid on his lap curled up. Neal's clothes were damp, they had dried a little bit even with it being overcast. The slight warmth from the puppy in his lap was the only bit of comfort he had. He dozed off thinking that his Pa and brother would come for him tomorrow.

At sundown the second day, Neal was sick with hunger. He thought a drink of water would be better than food. Even as thirsty as he was, he wouldn't drink from the muddy flood water. The water had only dropped a slight bit from where it was the first day that he took refuge in the tree.

Neal couldn't remember if it had been three days, or four. He was starting to have things become foggy in his brain. Neal started to talk to his brother aloud. He was telling him that he couldn't wake up.

"I'm dreaming Kenny, my dream won't let me wake up, is that you… put me on my horse."

It was at this point that Neal could feel somebody moving him. "It must be Pa, Kenny," he was saying "He found me in my dreams." Someone laid him down. "Thank you, Pa… I knew you would come."

CHAPTER 2

NEW BEGINNINGS

Neal had woken up in a hut. The hunters of the Otoe-Missouria, native people had found him. They were the people of the river mouth, known as the people of the wooden canoes. He was suffering from hunger, dehydration, and having delusions as well. It took them several days to nurse him back to good health. The women and children of the tribe took care of Neal while some of the others searched to return him to his people. After many attempts to find his people, to no avail, they decided to raise him as one of their own. As the children of the tribe teach Neal how to speak their Language.

When he was fully accepted, they gave him the name of River. Adopting both River and his puppy named 'Pup'. He spent several years with the tribe and earned his way in it as well. At the age of 16, he found his place with the hunters. By the time he was 18, he was considered to be one of their finest hunters. Pup joined him the year they left to hunt bison, being able to hold his own as well. The next year, after the hunt was finished River and the hunters had the meat and hide ready for the return to the village when in the distance, they saw a wagon train. At this time Neal was

The leader of the hunters spoke to River in English. "You can no longer be with us." Neal didn't like to hear it. "You have grown strong, and learned much…" He gestured to the wagons. "But now you must join your people. You have completed your journey with us. Live well River. We cannot welcome you anymore. Go… be with your people now."

Knowing their people's way and how the chief was, he knew he must do as told. He had no choice in the matter but knew it was for the best.

"Be well my brothers, I will repay your lessons, as I live and breathe." He nodded to them all, raising his bow high, Neal then departed for the wagons.

Neal's apparel was that of the Indian. He rode in on a horse and led the second one that was packed with his share of the bison in tow. When he approached the wagons, Neal rode off to the side, a distance away. As soon as a rider spotted him, Neal stopped his horses, he held his bow high. A second rider joined the first and moved to him carefully.

Neal spoke, "My name is Neal, I am a white man." He remained stopped on his horse. When the riders were several feet from him a man spoke to him.

"Did I hear you say that you were a white man?" The man was looking him over. Neal's hair was long and tied back with a leather string. He was shirtless and wearing a loin cloth and some tall moccasins.

"Yes sir," Neal replied. "I have brought meat. I ask to join you, as I haven't seen a white man in eight years or so." He pointed to the north. "They are the ones who found me and taught me from a small boy." Neal chose his words very care-fully. "Now that I have found my people, I can no longer live with them. That now I belong with my real people."

"Neal…" the same man spoke. "I am Charles, and you may join us. Bring your bounty, and follow us. We'll make camp soon."

Once again Neal felt his life starting over.

CHAPTER 3

THE LOST RIVER

That evening the folks of the wagon train made camp. All of them would look at him from time to time, but they didn't speak. "When you have eaten, I want all of you to meet with me here at the campfire," Charles said. "This man's name is Neal. He has brought us fresh meat." Charles then turned to Neal. "On this train, we all share our bounty, do you understand?"

"Yes sir, I do" Neal answered him. "There is plenty for each wagon to share." Most of them were taken by surprise that he spoke their language so well, considering he didn't look like a white man.

"Robert," Charles said. "Find a plate and cup for Neal."

After everyone had eaten, Charles stood up. "Neal…" He spoke. "I don't want you to feel awkward or uncomfortable, but the rest of us would like to hear your story… If you are good with telling us." He motioned for Neal to stand.

Neal told the story of a boy who left Kentucky with his family and was swept away by the big Mississippi flood. How Neal had found his 'pup' and how he had been saved and nursed to good health by the Otoe-Missouria. He told them that the people on this train were the first white people he had seen in around eight or more years.

"Do you remember your brother's name?" A voice rang out.

"My Brothers name was Kenny," Neal answered. "Kenny Morgan." The man who asked this came forward, and he just stood and stared at Neal. The man's face was paled. Neal watched as the first tear dropped from the man's eyes. The man was trying to speak.

"We tried to find you," The man choked. "Looked for weeks" His words struggled to escape his lips. "You are my brother, Neal, I am Kenny Morgan".

Neal was as shocked as his brother. Kenny hugged him, and they laughed and wept. The people on the train clapped their hands and cheered. Neal saw the ladies wiping their eyes.

"We have much to talk about brother," Kenny said as they both sat down.

"Get ready folks we roll at daybreak," Charles piped up. "Kenny, you and Neal take your time. Robert will ride your watch tonight." Before he walked away from them, he said "Try to get some sleep tonight. Neal… If you'll take it… I'll hire you on as an outrider."

Kenny looked at Neal. "Tell'em you'll take it." Neal nodded to Charles.

That night the two talked. Kenny told Neal that they had searched for him for 7 days. The ferry crossing had been washed away, by the flash flood he was taken by. Fifteen people died in it. The twenty-five head of cattle perished, but all their father's horses made it out. Including Neal's horse, alongside finding the rest of the herd. By the time they found his horse, it was caked in mud.

"Mom and Dad took it hard," Kenny told him sincerely. He paused a bit then continued. His voice cracked as he choked out the words. "I took it the worst kid... I never stopped blaming myself." Kenny sniffled in the dark. "But look at us now... You were the one who found me!"

Neal told Kenny about the puppy, now grown and at their feet. He told him that 'Pup' kept him company for three to four days until the Otoe-Missouria found him. Pup kept him from giving up. He told him about how he had been raised and learned the Osage tongue. How to hunt, fish, and gather as the Otoe-Missouria watched for the white men.

The moon was high when they rolled out their bed rolls. "Neal, I'll give you clothes in the morning." Kenny laughed. "The white men won't like it if you are walking around all day half-naked."

Before the sun was up the next morning, Charles gave Neal a shirt. It was soft and clean; Kenny gave him a pair of pants. The pants were a little too short, but when he put his tall moccasins on, no one could tell. "One of these evenings, a lady on the train can cut your hair for you," Kenny continued.

"Maybe... maybe not," Neal replied as he smiled.

Charles slapped him on the back and said "It's whatever you sort out kid." He was grinning. Neal's hair was pulled back and tied behind his neck. It hung to his waist. "Kenny..." Charles barked. "Show him the ropes, get mounted, and head out."

Neal had ridden in on a sorrel and led his grey Mustang. His sorrel didn't take to a saddle at first so it took a bit to settle him down. This was the beginning of another new life for him, but Neal was willing. He felt at home having his brother near him again. An empty place in Neal's soul seemed fulfilled.

From when the brothers had reunited, they had five days before they would reach the Flint hills and the tall grass of Kansas. Neal learned his job quickly and was accepted by everyone on the train. If they had no trouble, they would be at Fort Dodge in twenty days.

Over the next four days, Neal learned they would leave six wagons and twelve more would join their train in Baxter Springs Kansas. Two wagons would contain supplies for Fort Dodge.

The train's supply wagon was almost empty. So, on the last day in the Missouri territory wood was gathered for morning and evening campfires. Neal learned to shoot a rifle and revolver pistol. He taught the outriders different ways to track and the Indian way to check movement in the distances. Soon they crossed into the Kansas territory that they called a state.

The camp was made on the outskirts of Baxter Springs. Charles made his meeting short. "The six wagons leading the train will be led by the outriders into the settlement. You will all be given your land papers when you arrive." Charles told the settlers. "Our supply wagons will be filled here as well. In three days, we will be joined by ten new families. They'll come with us to Fort Dodge, then two more wagons with the fort supplies. Make camp and rest your horses. You are free to trade in Baxter Springs, However, you men should accompany your ladies if they want to go in. It isn't an entirely safe settlement. Everyone's Dismissed."

Charles had chosen Neal, Dan, and Cole to ride into Baxter Springs with the wagon folk that was leaving the train. Charles rode alongside them.

The wagons stopped in a line. When Charles dismounted, he handed his reigns to Cole. "You three boys wait here for me. I'll be back in a bit." Before he walked away, he said. "The ladies and kids on those wagons," He pointed in their direction. "They'll be without their men for a bit. Keep your eyes out for them." He walked to the lead wagon; the six men joined him. Then the seven men disappeared inside the bank.

Dan dismounted and adjusted his saddle. The three kept watches over the wagons. It wasn't long before Charles and the men joined the wagons. Neal watched Charles shake hands with each man then headed towards his outriders. Charles and Dan mounted.

"Well, boys." Charles grinned. "Let's head for the trading post." The four men tied their horses and entered the building.

Charles handed a list to the Lady behind the counter. The rest spread out looking over the goods. Neal felt uncomfortable. "Neal" Charles called out. "Step over here son."

"You've got pay coming." He said, "Will you let me help you find what you need?" Charles looked at him and could see his discomfort.

"That would be nice Sir…" Neal told him. "I haven't been in a place like this, ever, in my life." Neal looked around not knowing where to start.

"Then let's start in here son." Charles pointed the way. Walking up to a man behind the long counter. Charles greeted him. "Afternoon Sir." He motioned Neal up to the counter. "We'd like to look at your guns, gun belt, a six-shooter, maybe a rifle, and a saddle boot."

"We have no credit here sir." The man said it very plainly. Then looked up at Charles. "It's been a few months." They shook hands.

"We are all doin' well Poke," Charles replied. "I've got me a new outrider and he'll be needing a few things. He has pay coming. So, I'll take care of it." Charles smiled.

With their new supplies purchased, the four men filled their saddle bags, stepped into their saddles once more, and headed back to camp. Neal hadn't owned so many things in his life.

He had a gun belt, a six-shooter, a rifle, and a boot for it, Charles had chosen a set of large saddle bags and his bed roll. It was all wrapped up in a rain slicker. That included several boxes of ammo. The man behind the counter threw in a cup and a tin plate out of generosity. Neal also chose a knife and a sheethe for it.

A big meal was fixed that evening and a wagon rolled in, at mid-day. The camp folk shared their food with the newcomers. There was an older man, his daughter, and his granddaughter. His name was Pete Simmons.

The ladies of the trained welcomed the new women. Neal had run out of things to keep him busy. A few of the children looked bored and started throwing rocks into the river. "Hey kids" Neal called to them. "Would you like to learn a game?" They all came running. He squatted down and drew a circle on the ground as he explained the rules. Neal placed broken sticks around the circle he drew. "Your rock has to land inside the circle. If it bounces out, you are out, if it stays you get another throw. The last one to keep their toss inside the ring is the winner, and then the game starts over, so everyone can play again. So, everyone finds a small stone to claim as your own." The children scattered, each looking for their own special rock.

"I am impressed." A sweet voice broke Neal's thoughts as he watched the children search. Neal stood, as the girl approached smiling. "I am Lori Jade." She extended her hand. Neal took it and gave a nod and gentle shake. "It's not every day that I get to see a grown man take time to entertain children. Especially when they are someone else's children. It's… Refreshing."

"My name is Neal," he said. "They were bored, but still full of energy." Neal laughed. "Would you like to join us, Lori Jade?" Several children had found their stones, there were two still searching. "This game is the beginning of teaching them a skill."

"Teaching," Lori said. "Is what *I* do. Thank you, and I will kind Sir." She bowed. "I best find a stone."

The oldest boy was about 12. "Wow Neal," he swallowed. "She's real pretty." Neal laughed and ruffled his hair.

Lori returned with a stone, and the last two children in tow. "I have gathered our strays, Neal," she smiled. "Shall we begin?"

"Okay, kids." Neal had their attention, "I don't get to play, because I am the watcher of the circle." He winked at the youngest child. "I'll show you how to toss the stone, and then you each get two practice throws." Neal tossed his stone. It landed in the center of the circle.

"No fair!" one of the many boys complained.

"That is another reason I am the watcher of the circle." Neal laughed. "So now each of you gets to practice." Neal walked to the circle and retrieved his stone. All the children and Lori threw them one at a time. They used up all their practice throws and then the real game began. Six stones lay in the circle. The smallest boy's stone didn't reach the circle. He was out. "What's your name son?" Neal quickly asked him.

"It's Tod." The child said as he kicked his toe in the dirt. He was disappointed.

"Well, Tod," Neal spoke to him. "You get to help me now. You see," Neal spoke to his audience. "Each time the round is over, the watcher removes a stick. Like this." He showed everyone. "Then we move all these other sticks inside, and the circle gets smaller. Can you help me do this?" The boy's eyes lit up, and he nodded. Neal smiled and winked at Lori. She smiled and gave Neal a thumbs-up.

The two grownups played with the children for an hour or so, and then the meal was called. The children took off.

"Wait a minute, Tod," Neal called out. The small child stopped and turned to Neal. "You my friend get to guard the sticks for the game." Neal pulled a leather string from his pocket, tied the sticks together, and handed the small bundle to Tod. Tod looked up wide-eyed and proud. "Can you do this?" Tod grinned and took off. Neal stood.

"Shall we…" Lori smiled. She and Neal headed for the campfire.

That evening, the men folk checked the wagons. Kenny showed Neal what they were doing and why. Hubs were greased, and wheels were carefully checked along with every part of each wagon. The outriders were to help where they were needed. All repairs were made.

By the time the work was finished, coffee was ready and all the folks had gathered at the campfire. The men sat; they were still talking as the woman filled their cups. In a brief moment of silence. Young Tod climbed into Neal's lap. His mother started to scold him, but Neal quickly raised his hand and smiled at her "Neal" Tod asked. "Can you tell me a story about the 'injian' kids?" The ladies giggled, and Tod's mother sighed.

"What story would you like me to tell you, Tod?" Neal questioned the kid.

"Tell me about their school," He replied. "I get to go to school in a few years!" Tod stated proudly.

"Well then," Neal started his story and all the children on the train gathered around him. "The Otoe-Missouria are taught to pray every day. They pray to the Great Spirit. Now I believe that the one they call the great spirit is the one we call 'God'. They give thanks first thing each day. Thanks for the rising sun, and the moon. And for the earth beneath them." Neal paused.

"Are their schools big?" Tod curiously asked.

"They don't have schools in buildings or huts. We sat outside each day for our schooling." Neal Continued. "Everyone in the tribe taught us different things. We didn't have books. If it rained or snowed, we didn't have school… so to speak that day." The children around Neal scooted closer. "The elders, or old ones would talk about their elders and pass down the stories of things that had taken place long ago. This way nothing was forgotten." Lori filled Neal's cup with coffee. "Some of the mothers and fathers taught about things we would gather… for food… or our huts. The girls weren't allowed to hunt. The men had that job, but the girls and women were the bosses of our huts, our homes, and our camps. Neal looked down and Tod was asleep in his arms. When he glanced up Tod's Pa smiled and took him. He nodded to Neal.

"Go on… Go on!" the children attempt to coax Neal into telling more.

Neal hadn't realized it, but the entire camp was engrossed in his story.

"Do you miss them?" A young girl was asking

"No… not at all." Neal tapped his hand against his heart. "I will always carry them with me here." He sipped his coffee. "We were taught that each of us has a place on this earth, and our own trail to follow. So, when the hunting party I was with saw this wagon train… our leader knew it was the white men…

and he sent me away to be with my people." Again, Neal was lost in his memory. "I almost died… I was found by them… they took me in and taught me… but they always let me know that my place was not with them. That one day I would again be with my people."

"All right children…" A lady said sternly. "Tell Neal good night… It's time for bed now."

All the ladies took the children to the wagons except for Lori and her mother. "Let me see if I understand you properly Neal." Lori smiled and asked, "The women of the villages were the bosses?" The whole camp roared with laughter and chuckling.

"Yes, they were." Neal laughed with them. "You've heard of divorce? Well, if a man misbehaved, or if his eyes strayed so to speak…" He finished his coffee and continued. "His wife could… reject him… she would simply throw his things out of the hut he had built her. Then it was settled." Everyone was bellowing with laughter until Neal continued. "He could… and some did… woo them with gifts and kindness, then he could return. Only after he would re-marry her by a ceremony. But it didn't happen often. When they chose each other from the start, they loved each other, and usually stayed united until death."

"Son" Charles chimed in. "I'm having a vision." The camp listened in with anticipation including Neal. "I see that you will be telling stories around the campfire for days to come." The campers, with Neal, included chuckled and laughed as many conversations took over.

Lori refilled Neal's cup with coffee and put the pot back on the campfire. When she returned to his log, her cup in hand she sat next to him and spoke. "You sir, are a very good storyteller, and a natural teacher."

"I think it was because of how the Otoe raised me, they teach every day, almost all the time. That is all." Neal told her with a smile on his face. "They brought me home; I'll be forever grateful to them for that. I had carried an empty place inside of me for a long time. I thought my folks and my brother had died."

"Neal…" Kenny said to him. "I didn't realize that you had thought that." His voice was shaky. "We thought you had too." Kenny laid his hand on his brother's shoulder. "I am itching to get you back to the ranch outside of Dodge. Mom hasn't had a light in her eyes since you disappeared. I think, little brother, that you are going to put that spark right back into them!"

Early the next morning. Neal and Kenny had the campfires ready when Charles and Lori put their coffee on the coals at the side. "Don't get up boys," Lori demanded playfully. Having a small blanket around her shoulders she continued. "I'm going to squeeze between you two. I'm chilly, so you two are going to be my warmth."

"Kenny, Charles had told me you are getting married when we reach Fort Dodge." Neal prodded.

"I sure will," Kenny said smiling. "Mrs. Kenneth Morgan." He stretched and stood up.

"Hey!" Lori laughed. "You've caused me a draft."

Kenny walked up to the campfire, picked up the four cups, and returned with the pot. As he was filling the cups he said. "She is staying with the folks until I return." He took the pot back to the campfire. "Her name is Linda, she and Ma were making her a dress when I left. Ma said she would keep her busy while I was gone."

Lori had shivered. Neal swung his leg over the log to straddle it and pulled Lori against his chest as Kenny was sitting back down. Neal had then wrapped his arms around her.

"Nice." She cozily replied. "You are very warm Neal."

Charles chuckled at the both of them. "We could sit closer to the campfire child…"

"No…" she stated firmly. "This is nice, at the campfire, I'd have to turn myself around over and over." She chuckled. "Like a rabbit over a pit, but right now… I am warm all over." They all laughed. "When the sun comes up… then I will let go of Neal." She proudly stated.

"Hey." Neal snickered. "Now, who is holding who?"

CHAPTER 4

UNEXPECTED SURPRISES

During the next few days, the rest of the wagons joined the camp. Charles and two outriders went back to Pokes Trading Post and replenished the supplies for the wagon train.

The trees showed the season changing as their leaves were turning colors. Their beauty surrounded the camp. The next morning the wagons rolled westward. Eventually reaching the Flint Hills they made camp for the night. Charles had used this campsite many times. It was a regular route for him and it was familiar.

The wagons were circled and horses unhooked. They then hobbled the horses and let them out to graze. Picket lines were attached to each wagon, from one wagon to another to keep the horses from invading the camp. All the children ran and played, whilst the women prepared the meal.

That evening they shared stew and biscuits. A lady had made enough sweet bread for everyone. It was buttered and tasted of cinnamon. Before sunset, the camp was cleaned up and folks gathered around the campfires to visit. The outriders were chosen to watch for the night. Three were to watch until midnight. Then three from midnight until sunrise. Kenny, Gene, and Neal slept.

The children were gathered around Lori as she read them a story by the campfire. The story was about a young boy and a bean stock. The parents enjoyed the break from their children for adult conversation. Soon after, the folk slept.

Charles, Kenny, and Gene were at the campfire when Lori walked to the campfire that morning. The sun had not risen yet. She filled her cup. "Another chilly morning. I fear fall is upon us."

"The fresh riders just headed out." Charles chuckled. "Neal will be in shortly."

"I've never met anyone like him before," Lori said to Kenny. "He has captured my heart and he doesn't even know it." She giggled and the men laughed.

"Well… I think he knows it now." Neal was laughing.

"Those darn moccasins you wear!" Lori was blushing intensely "I think you could sneak up on a mountain lion." All the men were laughing.

"A person learns things when they are quiet." Neal laughed. He turned Lori away from himself and snuggled her back against his chest, wrapping his arms around her.

"I've known Lori's folks a long time Neal," Charles told him. "So, I'm not sure which of you I'll cheer for." Lori and all the men laughed. Kenny filled their cups with coffee, then returned the pot to where it came from.

The camp was abuzz as everyone hooked up the teams, cleared the camp, and the wagons rolled to the northwest.

In many places, along with the Sante Fe Trail, the route was easy to find and follow. Other places were not. Riding the tall grass, the outriders watched for washed-out land and gullies that would be hard for the wagons to pass through. The land could be rugged as well as dangerous. Neal learned that the rest of the outriders hired by Charles had been to Franklin Missouri and back to Fort Dodge many times. On each trip, they guided the wagons westward.

This trip was no different from the others. Some wagons would drop out as they arrived at their destinations along the journey. When this train had camped to the south of Wichita Kansas, some of the wagons would be at the end of their trip as they made it. The train in turn picked up a few more wagons that wanted to continue to Fort Dodge.

Kenny told Neal he thought they were five to six days out of Wichita as they rode. Kenny had already told his brother that his Pa had a ranch close to Fort Dodge. He and his Ma had done well. They started by selling horses to the Calvary. Their Pa would buy and trade horses, then break them for the soldiers.

"A short time later." Kenny told Neal, "We had bought a herd of cattle out of New Mexico, so now Dad provides beef for the Fort and a few nearby settlements. He's a fair man Neal, Pa could raise his prices, but he won't. He says that he does well and greed goes against the Lord." Kenny laughed. "Ma wouldn't stand for it either."

"I barely remember their faces, Kenny," Neal told him. "Sometimes, I can see Pa's face in my dreams."

The men rode on keeping their eyes on the trail. "I saw you ride in Neal," Kenny told him. "I didn't know who you were until you told your story. Your face in my mind was a 10-year-old kid. It was sorta frozen in there." Kenny swallowed back the lump in his throat. "You do look like Dad though; you are even tall like him. They may or may not recognize you Neal, but they will know you. I knew it was you as you told your story… I just knew."

They found the camp for that night and scouted around a bit. Everything looked to be undisturbed and sound. So the two headed back to join the train.

"Before we get back Kenny." Neal gave him a sideways glance. "What do you think about Lori?"

"She seems really nice." He responded. "Why are you asking me?"

"Back in the tribe, the girls did all the choosing and…" Neal stumbled for the right words. "Chasing." He cleared his throat. "Should I be returning her… actions?"

"Look, Neal…" Kenny was struggling not to burst out with laughter. "That's not our way. If you like her… You… sorta choose her too, then follow your gut, your feelings, your heart. Just don't be too pushy or forward. Start small, a few wildflowers, a handmade gift, most girls are happy to have a conversation." They were almost back to the train. "It's not one more than the other, it is an equal exchange." Kenny playfully slugged his brother's arm. "Take it one day at a time, you'll sort it out."

"All I want to do is scoop her up, and head for the hills." They both laughed hard.

"You two sound like a couple of giggly girls." Charles smiled, "How did it go out there?" Kenny stopped to give Charles a report. Neal rode on towards the train.

Neal rode up to Lori's wagon. Lori was handling the lines. "Afternoon folks." He winked at Lori specifically.

"We haven't seen you all day Neal." She smiled. "Thought Charles had maybe run you two brothers off."

"He sent us out on point today." Neal nodded to Lori's mom. "It's really pretty around here. Kenny and I have seen a lot of game today as well."

"Will your horse ride double?" Lori asked Neal. Surprised by the question he nodded in response. "Grandpa" Lori had started. "I'll be back in a bit." She handed the lines to the older man. Lori had stood up on her side of the seat and slipped herself onto the back of Neal's horse. When she felt comfortable behind his saddle, she wrapped her arms around his waist.

"I am sure you can't be cold." Neal teased.

"No." she laughed. "I've been waiting all day to do this though."

"Neal," Charles called out. Neal kicked his mount into a slow lope. Charles and Kenny were still mounted where Neal had left them. As he and Lori approached, Charles stated. "The three of you can go on to the campsite and start getting it ready."

"Oh good." Lori told him, "My backside has been ready to get off that wagon all day." Neal growled and the two of them laughed.

They could see the train approaching in the distance as they arrived at the camp. Neal climbed a tree and threw down some ropes. Not much left to do.

"Lori" Kenny started. "Do you mind me asking why you're going to Fort Dodge?"

"I don't mind at all Kenny." She was still on Neal's horse, fully in the saddle. "We're meeting my Pa there. I may also take a teaching position at the fort." She motioned for Neal as she responded. "Why do you ask?"

Neal was helping her off her horse as she said. "I couldn't reach the stirrups and a belly flop could have been quite embarrassing." While saying this Lori had locked eyes with Neal.

Kenny was watching the two and laughed as he replied. "Just curiosity I guess." He said as he walked away.

"Would you like to walk to the stream with me?" Neal asked. "After the camp is set up?"

"Do we have to wait that long?" Lori smiled.

"Girl," Neal growled. "You are killing me." They laughed and walked over to stand with Kenny.

By the time the wagons were set and the ladies were busy putting their biscuits on the coals, the children were running and playing. They were excited to be free from the wagons. Young Tod had found Neal while he cared for his horses. Lori joined them. Neal was roughhousing with Tod.

With Tod on Neal's back, Lori was playing too. Lori said. "I'm going to get you, Tod." As they laughed and played Neal suddenly froze in place.

Lori held onto Tod, "Tod you listen to me buddy you stay with Lori, do not follow me, do you understand?" Tod nodded as his eyes widened. "Stay put Lori… please."

Neal walked quickly out into the tall grass. Lori stepped to the side to see where Neal was going. "Shush…" Lori told Tod. "Be really still."

The evening was cool, Neal had pulled on his Indian shirt. With his long hair tied behind his neck, he looked similar to the three Indians on ponies standing not far away. Neal stopped when he closed the distance between them. They were hunters. They waited calmly.

Neal spoke to them and used wide hand and arm gestures. One of the hunters spoke to Neal. Lori didn't understand the language. In about a 10-minute span the men spoke to each other. "Charles is coming Lori," Tod whispered. Lori couldn't take her eyes off Neal.

The Indians had five horses and three riders. Lori was sure the fourth horse had a body tied down on it. The fifth horse was empty.

"Do you know what this is about Lori?" Charles whispered to her.

"Shush," Lori whispered. "Neal isn't nervous or doesn't seem worried, I think they might be friendly."

A few minutes later. The Indian mounted, Neal gave him an arms embrace of sorts, and the horses and riders rode away.

Neal strode up to Lori and Charles. He plucked Tod out of Lori's arms and took her hand into his. "We need to get back to camp Charles," Neal calmly told him, as he was taking great strides. "An injured cougar is on the loose and he's close." Neal was practically dragging Lori along and she tripped in the tall grass. Neal shoved Tod onto Charles's shoulders. "I'm sorry babe." He told Lori. Then scooped her up bridal style into his arms.

Neal could see fear in her eyes. He lowered his lips near her ear. "I've been wanting to hold you like this all day." He smiled, Lori, relaxing a little and giggling.

"Gather around folks," Charles shouted out.

"Make sure you have your kids with you," Neal added. Then placed Lori on her feet.

"Is everyone accounted for?" Charles asked loudly. All the folks looked around and nodded.

"We've had a few visitors." Neal began. "A small Sioux hunting party. They were taking a 14-year-old boy back to their camp… south of us. Their boy had been attacked and killed by a cougar…" Everyone was suddenly rigid as stone with an eerie silence surrounding them.

"It's a large male cougar." Neal continues. "The cougar is wounded, the boy put a knife in his chest as he fought for his life. One of the hunters said they tracked it, but then lost its trail in the grass. If any of you don't know this, this will make that cougar twice as dangerous."

Charles had taken over at this point. "Keep the young ones close. I usually only keep six, but now I have seven outriders. I'll need at least four more watchers tonight, for the safety of all of us. Everyone, please make sure to check your guns, and keep 'em fully loaded and ready." Then he finished with. "Let's eat, and stay close to one another."

The moon was bright but still low in the sky by the time camp was packed up and ready for the morning. All the folk in the wagon train made it back to their wagons. Six men were watching the horses. All the outriders were leaving camp to take their positions outside the circle of wagons. Neal had walked Lori and her folks to their wagons.

As fast as a bolt of lightning, Neal's horse's back arched as it reared up, snorting and jumping sideways. The cougar was in mid-air, with its intent being locked on Neal. Lori let out a horrified scream as Neal grabbed the cougar by its sides and jerked its body down against him with all his strength. Neal crashed the cat's back into the ground beneath his body. Neal could feel the butt end of the knife the boy had lunged into the cougar pressed against him. Then he aggressively shoved the cat, causing the blade to press further in. Neal stood quickly and drew his six-shooter at the large cat as it twitched on the ground.

Before he could even think of pulling the trigger there was a loud BANG. Lori's grandpa shot the big cat as it now lays limply before them.

"I think you had already killed that cat, Son." Lori's grandpa stated.

Looking down at the cougar that lay limply at his feet, he could see the knife was what did it in. Looking at it closer it had gone through the cougar's heart.

"I was just making sure it was dead." Her grandpa chuckled as Charles joined in with laughter.

Everyone came out of their wagons. Even the outriders came into the circle. Dan was the first to comment. "I've seen some big cats before... But none as big as this one."

Lori's mom fussed about the blood on Neal's shirt. She made him strip it off. Lori not missing a beat covered him with a quilt. While looking him over she made sure he didn't have any injuries. The blood on Neal was from the wounded cat, and after cleaning that up, all that was left on him was purple and red bruises on his chest.

"Coffee is ready you two," Charles called out. Neal sat straddling the big log. He pulled Lori down to do the same and snuggled her against his chest. He wrapped the quilt close around them. "Son..." Charles started. "You've got more... nerve... man... that was quick as a flash of lightning." He filled their cups. "Dan's skinning out your cat," Kenny said. "Look at this." He held out the knife that they pulled out of the cat. Kenny had cleaned it up. Neal let the quilt drop, then stood and covered Lori's shoulders with it. He walked to the campfire and slowly turned the knife in his hand. Lori could see unshed tears in his eyes. Neal sniffed and blinked back the tears.

"This knife was a gift from his father. It was for his first hunt. This symbol is for the boy, this one is for his father." Neal stood shirtless in the cold night air. "After his first hunt is complete, his father will notch the handle." Neal showed each of them the handle. He walked back to Lori; she stood and covered him with her quilt. He picked her up as he sat down, then placed her on his lap.

"Neal," his brother said. "That's a sad thing. I can see you are thinking this out."

"I'll take it to the hunting party," Neal said. "At first light. Maybe I can catch them before they take the boy back." Dan refilled their coffee cups.

Neal was gone before the sun had even started to rise. He had the big cat's head in a cloth sack. He had tied it closed with a leather string. The boy's knife was tied to it on the outside. Traveling in the direction the hunter pointed, he let his horse find them. When Neal could see their small campfire, he called out to the hunters. Then he rode into the camp. He dismounted and handed the sack to the man he had spoken to the day before. Neal made sure the hunter could see the boy's knife. He prayed for the Sioux to the great spirit, then mounted his horse and left them.

When Neal returned to the wagons, the sun was close to breaking the horizon. "Neal Morgan…" Lori broke into his thoughts. "I have our coffee ready." She rose on her tiptoes as she pulled his face down and kissed him tenderly. Neal smiled as he looked into her eyes. Lori winked at him.

"Break it up you two." Kenny laughed.

"Big brother… You're messin' with my moment." The three laughed.

CHAPTER 5

MERGING FAMILIES

After the morning that Neal returned the boy's knife, he and Lori were never apart unless he was on duty or sleeping. Some days when he was on duty, she would ride alongside him. The wagons camped on the outskirts of Wichita, and Charles rode with the wagons that were leaving the train. Kenny, Cole, and Ben accompanied him. Supplies were ordered and others were purchased that day.

"Hey, Charles," Kenny called out. "Would you try this on?" Kenny was holding a heavy winter coat. "Neal's birthday is tomorrow. He's bigger than me. You gave him a shirt that fit, so if this will fit you, I'm gonna get it."

"Neal hasn't said a word about his birthday," Charles told him.

"Thing is," Kenny said. "I don't think he remembers. Mom always made a fuss when we were young. But that has been a lifetime ago for him."

"Well then…" Charles grinned. "How about we put our heads together and make a fuss." The four men laughed.

The next morning, November 1ˢᵗ, Neal was up early as usual. He and Lori were cuddled in the quilt next to the campfire. They sat close enough Neal could reach the coffee pot.

"Are you making plans for us in that head of yours Neal?" Lori asked.

"I am babe." Neal turned her around in his lap to face him. "I was hoping you might like to be my wife." She had her eyes locked into his. "When I close my eyes at night, I see your eyes, and my arms miss you." He told her. "What about you… Have you made plans for us?"

Lori pulled herself into Neal's chest. "I think my plans are the same as yours." She sighed. "Just wondering; how long before you ask me out right?" Neal's body shook beneath her as he laughed. "I love you Lori, will you marry me?"

"Yes!" she answered. "Thought you'd never ask." Lori rolled her eyes, and they laughed again. "Neal…" she said in a soft and meaningful way. "I love you too."

Neal stood, folded the quilt in half, and then wrapped it around Lori. "I am going to check the horses, if you want to come along, go grab your coat." While he waited for her by the campfire she got her things.

After he finished with the horses, they returned to the campfire. "If it weren't for my feet Neal, I wouldn't get so cold," Lori told him. "Maybe I need warmer socks." She laughed, watching Neal turn around. "You look like a rabbit on a spit." She told him. "Round and round." They both laughed. "How about we go to the settlement and get you a warm coat?" Lori sincerely suggested.

"Can't do that," Kenny said as the men returned. "Happy Birthday brother." Kenny smiled as he handed his brother a brown-paper-wrapped package.

"Birthday…" Neal looked up at him. "Is it really my birthday? or are you just ragging me?"

"Neal… today is November 1st," Kenny said. "It's your birthday."

Neal opened the package and shook out the coat. Then slipped into it. "Thanks, Kenny… It's a good fit. It's really nice."

Neal put his finger on Lori's cold pink nose. "You wait here, I'll be right back." Then he kissed her in front of God and the men.

Lori blushed and then started handing out coffee cups to the men. A few minutes later Neal returned. "I made these for you a while back," Neal told her. Neal sat Lori down on the log and pulled her boots off. Then slid her feet into tall moccasins.

"These are wonderful!" She wiggled her toes. "My feet already feel warmer." Lori was looking at her feet.

"Wait… what…?" Kenny said, "You weren't going to give those to her until…" Kenny turned to Lori, then back to Neal. "She said yes?"

Neal was beaming. "We haven't set a date yet, but Lori said she'd marry me." He pulled Lori to her feet. "But first I need to ask her Pa… I wanna do this right."

"Well darn," Lori said playfully. "I was hoping we could get a preacher in Wichita." They all laughed.

Lori's mom and grandpa had walked up behind the men. Her mom placed her hands on Lori's shoulder and smiled at her.

"Y'know Neal," Lori said. "My Mom and Grandpa… They know you already." She was flirting with Neal. "You could get their blessings instead… Pa wouldn't mind, then we could get a preacher out here today." Getting on her tiptoes, she kissed him.

"I've seen you two cuddled in those quilts." Lori's grandpa announced. "N' all that kissin' going on." Neal didn't know what to say. "Way her mom and I see it, we were a thinkin' you need to make an honest woman out of my little girl here." Then the men joined together teasing Neal.

"Well… Mr. Simmons, Mrs. Jade…" Neal was a little nervous. "I'd do it in a heartbeat, … if you are sure that her Pa wouldn't skin me."

"Charles." Mr. Simmons chuckled. "Send someone to fetch the preacher, while I'll get my shotgun." Laughter erupted from the camp as whooping and hollering were heard far and wide. Meanwhile, Neal pulled Lori up close. "Getting married on my birthday would make it hard to forget our anniversary." He smiled and then kissed her.

Charles gave use of one of the empty supply wagons to Lori and Neal. The six outriders would share the other one. He sorted it out with the boys, who were good with this decision. They decided to have two sleep, as one drove, leaving three outriders mounted. The six of them would rotate.

Before the preacher arrived, the covered supply wagon seemed to be filling up with gifts from the other folk on the train. "We want you to have this feather mattress, we need the room it takes up." One had said. "I don't have use for this Dutch oven." Replied another. And so on, it went.

Lori's mom, grandpa, and outriders rode back from the settlement with a few things as well. Blankets, a coffee pot, and most importantly some warm socks for Lori. "And Neal…" Mrs. Jade said to him. "Today is the day you will be referring to us as mom… and grandpa." He hugged her gently and then said that he most certainly would.

"Charles" Tod's mother called out. "I need you to confirm sir." She asked him. "Do you want me to make a birthday cake or a wedding cake?" She was smiling coyly, but sincere.

"If you could do both, I'll replenish your supplies," Charles said with a proud smile, as everything was getting arranged.

The afternoon was warmer than the morning had been. Lori stood with Neal and the preacher. In attendance were all the folks she had grown to love. During the journey across the land here on the Santa Fe Trail. She wore a blue lace shawl over her shoulder. It matched the color of her eyes. To her, … it was the perfect wedding. "I'd like to introduce everyone to, Mr. and Mrs. Neal Morgan." The preacher was saying. "You may kiss your bride."

There was plenty of dancing and lots of food. The children ran about and played with one another. The day was very lively and everyone had a lot of fun. The wedding and birthday cake was enough to go around.

Before the sun had set that night a few more wagons had joined the group. They would rest a few days before continuing on to Fort Dodge.

That night Neal and Lori made love to each other, it was tender, gentle, and quiet. As they lay together in the wagon, they were warm and quiet. Lori was snuggled into Neal's arms. "Neal… promise me we will never go to bed angry with each other." She spoke. "I promise I will share my worries and good feelings, and everything in between with you. Promise me you will do the same, Neal."

"I promise," he told her. Neal was quiet.

"I can tell you have something on your mind." She said as she lay in the darkness. "Please, Neal… don't break our promises to each other." Neal felt her warm tears fall onto his chest.

Neal sat up and pulled Lori up with him. He pulled their quilts around them to keep her warm. "Babe…" He began. "I'm the happiest man on earth right now. But I do have some worries though." He held her close. "I work as an outrider. This is the last train on the trail until late spring. We have no land. No home. Not even a tipi." He chuckled. "My worry is… how do I take care of you… of us… that my beautiful wife is what is going on in my head. I have no regrets sweetheart; I'm only trying to sort this out." Neal sighed and kissed the top of her head.

"When we reach Fort Dodge," Lori said. "My Pa acquired land somewhere close by. Your folks have some land there too, so if you like it around there, maybe we could live there too."

Neal thought it over. "If you like it babe, we will. But make sure." He told her. "I can live anywhere as long as I know it pleases my wife."

"I feel the same way Neal," She purred. "As long as we are together. Pa doesn't live on his land. He will when he retires, I think Ma says he'll retire about a year from now."

"What does he do?" Neal asked. "Where does he work?"

Lori laughed. "I guess we've never talked much about my Pa… He's the General at Fort Dodge."

Neal laid down on his back, and his body began to wiggle and shake as he laughed deep from his belly. He couldn't hold it back; Lori was sure that the entire camp would hear him. He was roaring.

"What?" Lori started laughing as it was almost contagious. "What is so funny Neal?"

In between fits of laughter, Neal finally sputtered out. "I can see it now…" He was trying to catch his breath. "Your Pa will have me before a firing squad…" Neal roared, "You didn't ask me for her hand, he'll say." After Neal imitated some gun sounds, the two of them laughed until their sides hurt.

As they were finally quieting down. They heard an outrider approach their wagon. "You two love birds trying to start a stampede?" It was Kenny.

"Sorry Kenny," Lori said. "Neal has a busted funny bone." She giggled again. "See you in the morning."

Neal pulled Lori's back against his chest and they soon fell asleep.

CHAPTER 6

RESURFACING THE PAST

Before the sky turned grey the next morning, Neal and Lori had two pots of coffee on the coals. The outriders had just come into the circle.

"Man, that smells good," Dan said.

Kenny was right behind Dan, as he inquired. "Has Charles been around yet Neal?"

"Just now getting here fellows." They turned around to see Charles joining them.

Lori handed each of the men a cup of coffee as they sat down and gathered around the morning campfire.

"A dispatch rode up a few minutes ago." Kenny handed Charles a letter. The five of them get comfortable on their chosen logs as the campfire warmed them against the cool dewy breeze.

Charles read the papers. "The entire Walnut Valley could hear you two laughing last night." Dan chuckled to the newlyweds. "The thing is when you laugh Neal… folks might not know why you are laughing… but it makes everyone else start laughing." Kenny winked at Dan. Dan continued. "Your laugh, it's contagious… so to speak."

Lori giggled remembering. "He was picturing my Pa standing him in front of a firing squad for not asking for my hand." The four of them were laughing again. "Neal sort of lost it." She finished.

"As we were on watch, you two had a few of the wagons laughing right along with the rest of us." Kenny chimed in.

"Kenny…" Neal said. "Did you know her Pa is the General at Fort Dodge?"

"Your Pa is Lucas?" Kenny asked Lori, and she nodded in response with a smile on her face. "Your Pa has the land that connects with our land." Neal was standing there listening to Kenny speechlessly. "Both our dads are working out a plan together for the future. Kenny slapped his leg. "Now you two meet… and get married… not even knowing this." He laughed again. "The angels in heaven above must've brought it all together."

Lori kissed her husband and lovingly said. "This… was just meant to be."

Charles finished his letter and had been sitting quietly. "Speaking of your father Lori, this letter is from him." He said holding up the papers. "Looks like we all will be having company today… and lots of it." Charles stood. "Outriders… spread the word, we are having a meeting, midmorning today. Everyone on the train will be required to attend.

"Yes sir," All seven outriders responded.

Lori kissed her man again. "I'll be helping with the food and children until you return." She watched as the men walked away with Charles.

Midmorning after the camp had settled down, and everyone had gathered around, Charles started the meeting immediately.

"Folks" He began. "I've received word this morning that the Calvary will be joining us on the trail. Seem they are needed at the fort west of Dodge. Outriders, your jobs will be the same except my men will ride days only. They are providing our night watch for us. The Calvary," He continued. "Will take meals when we do. They are also providing their food and supplies along with the four men who will cook it. We'll have eight wagons of folks joining us to Fort Dodge and a total of sixty Calvary Men. There will be ten Calvary wagons, and we will make everyone feel welcome. Outriders, you'll each have extra riders with you each day. Before any questions are asked," Charles sipped his coffee. "We are not expecting any trouble this side of the Fort. The Calvary is headed the same way, and insists on escorting us." Charles grinned. "It may or may not have anything to do with the fact that we have the General's Wife, Daughter, and Father-in-law, with us. Any questions?"

"Oh boy!" Tod yelled. "Soldiers!"

"Charles," Lori asked. "Will I still be able to ride with Neal and Kenny along the way?"

"You may sweet girl." He told her. "We aren't expecting trouble, just a big increase in size." He smiled again.

As Neal walked to their wagon, he noticed Lori and her mom engaged in conversation. Lori didn't look happy. Her mom was trying to soothe her. He put his coat away and pulled his leather Indian shirt over his head. Then pulled his ponytail out. As he was close to joining the women, Neal heard Lori say.

"I'll not have it, Mom. I have Neal, and I won't be suffocated." As she turned, she walked into Neal's chest.

"Hey… hey babe," Neal said. "What has got you upset?" He glanced at his mother-in-law. She shook her head and then, rubbed her temples.

"Okay…" Neal said. "Which one of you want to share?" He turned Lori to him. "We made a promise to each other babe."

"She will tell you, Neal," Donna told him. "Just give her a minute to collect herself." Neal saw Lori glance around. He took her by the hand and then helped her into the back of their wagon.

"Last night, you asked me what was going on inside my head. "Neal told her softly. "Now, I want to know Lori, what's going on in yours?"

Lori told Neal how her father always had soldiers guarding her. Most of it he understood. He felt protective of Lori. But he let her talk. To and from everywhere she had gone, there was always someone around. As she reached the end, she locked eyes with Neal and swallowed hard.

"I hate not being able to enjoy a free moment. What my folks don't know… I never told them…" Lori couldn't seem to speak. Neal took her into his arms. "The last guard he put on me… almost raped me." Lori became silent as she was trapped in her memories.

When she spoke again it was a soft haunting whisper. "I bit him hard on his neck… he screamed and cursed at me… Dad's Sergeant had come into the stables. He saved me… He had seen the man slapping me because I bit him… The Sergeant nearly beat him to death… I wished he would have… That man… He almost took my innocence. The Sergeant was older than my Pa. He comforted me… He told me that I wouldn't have to tell anyone. That he would keep my secret." Lori sighed and laid her head on Neal's chest.

Lori's tears fell silently. Neal held her close. "You were the first man that I've ever been with like that Neal. That Sergeant thought my guard had taken me. I was so frightened that I never told him differently. Soon after, I left for school and haven't been back to the fort or seen my Pa since."

"Oh, babe..." Neal continued to hold her. "Men like that should be hung. No woman deserves to go through something like that." He sighed. "And about last night… You were my first too." He pulled her chin up so she had to look into his eyes. "Now that we are married, your Pa won't need guards for you... He'll see that all you need is me."

"It was only that one man." She told Neal. "He was creepy… he spooked me, and it turned out that it was someone like him, that Dad was trying to protect me from."

"It won't be the same now babe." Neal comforted her. "I promise you this… So now, I want you to trust me on it… can you do this babe… for both of our sakes?"

"I do feel safe with you… I guess we can't stay here and cuddle all day." Lori giggled

"Grrr" Neal growled. "You are killing me, girl." As they left the wagon he said. "You need to talk to your mom babe… You were a little sharp with her… just let her know that you are fine and that the two of us have sorted things out." Lori smiled and nodded.

A short time later Lori had the children help gather firewood for the camp. Neal helped the men grease and repair wagons, then tended the horses. The ladies in the camp made extra biscuits and cooked beef. Everything was ready for their sixty guests.

Midday the Soldiers arrived along with a few more wagons of families. Charles had called a meeting and made the men feel welcome. He announced to the Calvary that the train had prepared for them and they would be providing the evening meal. Everyone was dismissed.

An officer approached Charles. "I have a letter sir for Mrs. Jade. I am to deliver it in person. Could you introduce me to her?"

Lori and Neal stood up from the log. 'Pup' was at their feet. "I'll do it, Charles, if you wouldn't mind," Neal said. Charles nodded.

"This way sir," Neal said to the Soldier. Lori was by his side, when they reached the wagon Lori called her mother out by name.

"Mrs. Jade." She called out. "A Soldier to see you, ma'am" Neal helped his mother-in-law down from her wagon. "We've escorted him to you, from Charles."

"Thank you," The soldier said to them. "That will be all" Neal winked at Mrs. Jade. He and Lori had just been dismissed.

"May I help you, young man?" Lori's mom said to the Soldier.

'I've brought a letter from the General for you, ma'am," he told her. "It's a private matter. If you'll please excuse your guests."

"Young man," Mrs. Jade addressed him. "Please let me introduce you to my… guests." She then gestured to Lori and Neal. "This is Mr. and Mrs. Neal Morgan. My daughter, and son-in-law. They may be present for this private matter." She gave him a stern look.

"Oh… yes ma'am, I didn't realize." He bowed slightly to her, and then to them. "You are to read the letter… then I am to answer any questions and await your instructions."

"Oh, Mother… may I?" Lori pointed to the letter.

"Yes dear… read it aloud, let's hear what your father has to say." Mrs. Jade responded.

The soldier was surprised and confused as this wasn't what he had expected.

Lori cleared her throat and sat on a wooden box beside the wagon wheel. 'Pup' put his head in her lap. "Dearest Donna, can't wait until your arrival. I hope the trip has gone well for you and Lori. Everything is ready for the two of you. You probably know by now that the troops will be escorting your wagon train. Most of these men have come from the East. They are needed west of here at Fort Wallace. Because there are so many of them, I have sent an assignment for four to guard Lori. Her protection is important to me. As you know, though they are in uniform, some lack manners. If she will stay near you. All will be well. Awaiting your arrival, love you Always, Lucas Jade."

"Mom, this needs to be handled now!" Lori all but screamed at her.

"Young man," Mrs. Jade said to the soldier. "When my daughter left three years ago, she was a child. Her father forgets this. She has a husband, and as you see, a temper. The guards will tend to my needs. But hear me well." Mrs. Jade stared him down and put her finger in his chest. "All of them… all four… will stay away from her and my son-in-law. Have I made myself clear?" The young man started to protest but stopped abruptly when she said. "Because if you don't do as I say… My report to my husband may not benefit any one of the guards he has assigned. Now…" She finished. "Do you understand?"

He nodded, "Okay then…" She commented after his brief statement. "This is my wagon. That is all you need to know; get your men and your gear. We will be eating shortly." She put her arm through Neal's, then Lori's. "I know you are listening, Dad, are you coming?" They walked to the circle.

Grandpa joined Lori and Neal on the log. "Poor mother," Lori said to them, "They are already crowding her."

"Baby girl," Grandpa said. "Your Ma can handle it, and herself. Besides," He smiled at her. "My work is now done, no more handling the lines, fixing, the wagon, caring for the horses." He laughed. "Shoot, I could climb in the back and take a nap!"

"Grandpa," Lori giggled, "You'll be bored by the end of the first day!" Neal was laughing too.

The meal that evening was a success, all the boys in blue felt honored. A small group of them stepped to the center of the circle with a fiddle player and a lively song was sung. The evening was one that they wouldn't forget.

Lori and Neal were sitting in a group of soldiers when one of the older ones, who looked to be in his late thirties was telling a story of a bear hunt that he'd been sitting in on. Dan disappeared for a few minutes. As the Lieutenant told his story and ended it, Dan said "Look at this Men."

He opened the skin of the big cougar Neal had killed that night back on the trail.

"Good Lord above!" The Lieutenant exclaimed. "I've got to hear the story on this one. Big cats are something I've seen, but none of this size."

"Neal," Dan says. "It's your story."

"I don't care to share it… Kenny" Neal gestured towards him.

"No… guys." Lori butted in. "I want to tell it. After all, *I* was right in the middle of it."

"Be my guest sweetheart," Neal said smiling. Lori had sat down in his lap and started to share the story from beginning to end, not sparing a single detail.

"Whew, wee!" One of the boys chuckled, "I'm afraid I would've made a mess of myself." A group of blue boys started whacking him with their hats, and laughter filled the air as it erupted across the valley.

"Neal," The Lieutenant said. "If you know some of the language and ways of the Indian, we'd be proud to sign you up for a year to scout for us. We're always looking for someone like that. What do you say?"

"Thanks for the offer, Lieutenant, but no… I'd rather not." Neal told him in a very calm manner. "But before anyone gets puffed up about my answer, let me explain myself."

"That's fair." The Lieutenant said.

"When I was ten, A big flood happened on the Mississippi River, and it washed me away. My family searched for me, but never found me. A tribe of the Otoe-Missouria found me close to death and brought me back to health, they didn't have to do it. They could have just left me in that tree to die." Lori stood behind him and untied his hair. "I wasn't a slave, I wasn't mistreated, they raised me and taught me all they knew. I earned my horses, knife, and bow. I earned a place with the hunters. The Otoe-Missouria are distant relatives of the Osage and the Kiowa." Lori had finished brushing out Neal's hair and sat in his lap.

"I have seen and heard about the other side, the wars, and the slaughter. I have learned that there is both good and bad, on each side white or red. It does go both ways. To speak each other's Language and communicate is the best way."

"I will help if I'm needed between here and Ft. Dodge. But I won't 'sign on.' I mean no disrespect sir but I will make my judgments. It's how I was taught. My folks don't know I'm alive. I need to see them and get re-acquainted. By signing on with you I wouldn't have the freedom to do that." Neal paused and started brushing Lori's hair. "You seem like a good man sir, however, my friendship and help when you need me is all I will offer at this time. But I'll take no pay for it."

The Lieutenant nodded. "Well," He said to Neal, "Do you know where your parents are?"

"That's the best part." Neal smiled at him at looked across to his brother. "I was in a hunting party with the Otoe when one of the hunters saw this wagon train. I was told by the leader that day that my people were found. That I was no longer needed nor welcome as their family. That my place was with my real people. Then he sent me away." Neal finished.

Kenny spoke up, he was remembering that day. He had described to them the encounter of when they met, and how out of all the odds things worked out the way that they did.

"Friend," The Lieutenant spoke. "Your story is both warming and chilling."

"The story isn't finished there." Lori cut in. "Neal and I were married yesterday. Then… After… we found out, that our Pa's are good friends and share land boundaries." Lori smiled, "His folks don't know he's alive and on his way to them, and that he has married their best friend's daughter. My pa doesn't know either."

"I know your Pa missy," A voice rang out from amongst the men in blue. The older man stood up and continued. "When we get to the Fort. Notta one of you is gonna spill the beans about these two. It is their surprise to do themselves." The man paused then and asked. "Is this understood gentlemen?"

"Yes Sir!" was coming out from every direction. Someone amongst them asked. "Who is her Pa?"

'Her Pa is General Jade." He paused again, "and Neal's Pa is Roy Morgan."

Lori was on her feet; her hands flew to his cheeks. "Dusty…" She choked, "Is that you?"

"Yes, child." In a rigid voice, he boomed. "You men find something to do for a few minutes." The soldiers scattered at the command.

Dragging Neal with her, she walked to her friend in Blue. "It's wonderful to see you again… Dusty… this is Neal." The men shook hands.

"So, I've heard." He laughed. "I've been sitting there watching you, and not believing these old eyes… You look well child… did school suit you?"

"It was awful." She laughed. "And it was wonderful… I'm a teacher now."

"Excuse me, Sir." Neal cut in. "I don't mean to interrupt babe," Neal kissed the top of her head and wrapped his arms around her. "You know my Pa?" At this point, Kenny had joined them.

"Yes son," Dusty grinned. "And your Ma… and this man right here." He shoulder-bumped Kenny.

"You see, Kenny is marrying my daughter as soon as we get back." Dusty laughed. "Looks like the good Lord is packing us all in tight."

"I must say, Dusty…" Kenny questioningly stated. "I am really surprised to see you here."

"Well Son, I was going to give you a sneak attack." He laughed, "Then I got caught up in that cougar story, and then the rest of it came tumbling out. I guess sneaking up on you is out." Dusty stepped forward and pulled off his hat. He looked up at Neal. "Mr. Neal Morgan," He chuckled. "If you'd allow me, I'd like to hug your bride."

Neal gave Dusty, Lori's hand. Dusty hugged her tight. When the embrace ended Lori said as she looked deep into Neal's eyes. "Neal, can you, and Kenny give us a few minutes?"

"Yes babe, we can." He told her, "I'll go and fetch us all some coffee." Then he kissed her and the two brothers walked away.

"Dusty…" Lori stammered searching for her words.

"Look, missy… You don't have to bring that up." Dusty told her. "I told you all those years ago to just…"

Lori cut him off. "No Dusty… you need to hear me… I need to say this to you… That man… he would of… he was going to…" She stammered again. "But he didn't get it done, I was fighting him hard… maybe it was the whiskey I could smell on him… but you need to know he didn't get that far. He didn't ruin me. He did beat me some, and he scared the life out of me. I'm just… I wanted you to know. I couldn't talk about it then and I never got another chance to tell you before I left for school. And to thank you for saving me, and not talking about it, I had no reason to feel shame, but it still shamed me. I needed you to know… That is all."

Dusty took her hand. "Missy… I'm glad he didn't. I am glad you got through it all. It is all in the past now. But to close that book… that beast who called himself a man, the one who hurt you. He's dead. He got drunk and pulled a gun on an offi-cer. I'm not sure that Satan himself let him through the gates of hell…" They were looking out into the darkness. "You know what missy?" Lori looked at Dusty. "You got yourself a real good man here! I wanna be present when this big reunion comes together." Dusty laughed loud and hard with a deep belly laugh.

When Lori and Neal cuddled into bed that night, Neal asked. "Did you get your business sorted out with Dusty?"

"How did you know it was him?" She turned to face Neal. "I never told you his name."

"You didn't have to babe…" Neal pulled her close. "I could read it on both of your faces."

"I told him, Neal." She spoke. "The whole story. He said he felt better for me knowing. He said that man shouldn't have even touched me. He also told me that the man was killed in a gunfight. Then Dusty said he believed Satan wouldn't let a man that bad even into hell."

"Dusty is a good one," Neal told her.

CHAPTER 7

EMBRACING CHANGES

The next morning was pleasant, not warm, but not cold. Lori filled her coffee pot with water and sat it on the coals to heat. Neal was having coffee at the campfire with his brother. When it seemed hot enough, she used a glove and lifted the pot. "Neal, would you help me a minute?" She was walking to the wagon. "Could you lift that pail into the back of the wagon for me?" He did. "Now pour this into it for me please." She had sat the hot pot down. He did as she asked of him.

"What are you up to?" Neal asked her, as she climbed into the back of the wagon.

"I dear man, am going to take a bath." Lori blushed as Neal grinned.

"I should help you." He said and climbed in after her. Lori had washed and rinsed her hair, then wrapped it in a wool shawl. The covered wagon was closed up tight so she wasn't worried about being seen.

She sat on a quilt at the end of their bed and undressed. Dipping her clothes in and out of the warm water, quickly bathed herself.

"You my beautiful wife, have a body that's been made by the angels," Neal told her.

"And you my peeping husband are distracting me. My cheeks are going to be permanently red." He laughed. "Now hand me your shirt. I'm chilled, all I have left is my feet."

Neal tossed her his shirt; it was very long on her. Lori slipped it over her head and began washing her feet. "I will be having visions of you in my head like this all day girl." He laughed.

When she finished, she grinned at Neal. He could see pure orneriness dancing in her eyes. "Now my love," she stated with a loving tone "It is your turn."

Neal didn't wash his hair, but he stripped down and bathed himself.

"Not fair," Lori said blushing. "You aren't embarrassed one bit." She giggled and took off his shirt, then gave it back to him. They dressed and left the wagon.

Everything was loaded into the wagon that evening except the coffee pots and cups. The wagons would all roll out in the morning.

The wagon train left the Walnut River that morning and traveled all day. Later afternoon they arrived at the camp on the west banks of the Arkansas River. They had no problems occur that day. The warm weather had stayed with them. Neal handled the team's line all day.

Their family was all at the campfire together that evening. "Mom," Lori said, "When exactly is Pa going to take his retirement?"

"He mentioned either June or July." She answered. "I can't be for sure, but it's about that time, why do you ask dear?"

"There was some talk about ranching," Lori replied. "I just haven't figured it out yet."

"Mrs. Jade…" Kenny spoke. "I could answer for you if you'd like." She nodded.

"Our Pa had been buying and raising horses for the calvary… and others Lori," Kenny told her. "Your Pa and ours have talked about for three years now, raising beef for the Calvary as well. The two of them have put their heads together to accomplish this goal. Your Pa can't do either until he retires, the government won't let him. It's legal reasons of some kind. So, our fathers together plan on raising cattle and hay. They'll keep some for both of them. But at the same time keep Fort Dodge in steady supply. The business between them has been coming together as planned. Then when your Pa retires. He will buy in half with my Pa"

"Will I be able to work there Kenny?" Neal asked. "Lori and I will be needing a home… and everything else we will need."

"Neal… you are already a part of it." Kenny folded his arms across his chest. "The two of you will need to figure out which side of the Morgan or Jade boundaries to build your house. Other than that, the work and the pay are waiting for you."

"But you," Neal said. "You work for Charles…"

"I do Neal." He explained. "But I've only ridden for him on the last train each year. I signed on with him for this trip before Linda and I fell in love. I had already committed. Linda understood, plus Charles knows this is my last ride." Kenny's look was honest and knowing when he said. "I wasn't going to ride… I was going to tell him I had changed my mind… but this… all of it… Me and you, Lori and our Pa's… it was just meant to be like this. And you my brother are bringing the light back into our mom's heart. Good night, everyone… I'm turning in."

"Well… Lori." Neal said. "Looks like I got a job for us!"

Lori added. "Now all we'll need is a place."

"Lori dear," Her mom was smiling. "Your pa has built a house." She patted Neal's leg." We can't move there until he retires, by that time the two of you will know where you'll build yours, if, you want to set your roots down there."

"Thanks, Mom," Neal said, "The two of us will be sorting it out." He winked at Lori.

Two days later they were headed for the camp at the North Fork Creek. Neal and Lori were near the end of the train. As their wagon cleared the top of the rise and started down the long easy grade of the trail. They were amazed at the view. The train was stretched out well over a mile and they could see the wide blue-stem prairie around them.

They could see the soldiers spread out escorting them, and the tall waving grass in the bright sun.

"If I could paint a picture, Neal," Lori claimed. "It would be this."

They had just pulled the wagons into the circle when the Lieutenant rode up to them. "Neal, we have a dozen Indians just outside of camp. Could you lend me a hand?"

His horse was saddled, still tied to the back of the wagon. Neal was mounted pretty quickly. "Soldier" The Lieutenant ordered. "You and another man take care of this wagon." Then he and Neal took off.

"Well, 'Pup'" Lori scratched the dog's ears. "Looks like it's just me and you now, let us go find you some water."

Neal and the Lieutenant rode over the rise and there were ten calvary men side by side sitting on their horses. About a hundred yards away were about twelve Indians on their horses.

Neal reached to the back of his saddle, grabbed his bow, and lifted it high in the air, two Indians rode out. Neal said. "Just you and me Lieutenant, let your boys know."

"Stand in place men," The Lieutenant ordered.

He and Neal moved toward Indian riders and Neal Informed the Lieutenant. "However, many the Indians send is all you are allowed to send in return. It means they want to talk, and you want to talk. If you send out more than they do, it's a hostile act."

"Good to know my friend." He replied.

"Keep your hands off your weapons too, if you'll notice my bow is hung," Neal added.

The four riders all stopped when they were about three feet from one another.

Neal spoke in the Otoe tongue he said. "Otoe… Osage… Sioux… Kiowa." The other Indian spoke. Neal stepped down from his horse. "Stay mounted Lieutenant," Neal said.

One of the Indians dismounted. Neal spoke, his hands and his arms danced out sign language, then the Indian spoke, he had done the same. Back and forth, one then the other. Close to about fifteen minutes had passed. Then the Indian pulled a leather string from his headband and handed it to Neal. Then Neal pulled a pouch from his pocket and placed something in the Indian's palm. The Indian took a second look at Neal's exchange and spoke to him. Neal answered. Before they had parted there was a handshake of sorts but the grip was on each other's bicep, and then a nod from each man then they mounted to join their own men.

"Impressive," The Lieutenant said. When they reached their soldiers, Neal stopped.

"We need to all turn now and ride back to camp," Neal stated.

"You heard him men," The Lieutenant barked out.

When they rode up to their camp Neal spotted Charles and motioned to him. Neal dismounted as did the Lieutenant. "Charles you'll probably want to call up the outriders for this," Neal told him, "Would you like me to do it?"

"Now wait just a minute Neal." The Lieutenant started as he reached for his arm. "You can't…"

Neal cut him off sharply. "I don't work for you, buddy." Neal heard Charles telling Dan to gather up the outriders. "I work for Charles; I will tell you what was said. I suggest that you go fetch your officers and we'll talk at the campfire." Neal jerked his arm free from the Lieutenant. He and Charles walked to the campfire in the circle.

The folks of the wagon train began to gather around.

"You folks just go about your business." The Lieutenant ordered. "This isn't a public meeting."

"Charles…" Neal looked over at Charles.

"Lieutenant." Charles's voice sounded angry.

"You sir," Charles was in the Lieutenant's face. "Are in charge of all these men in blue, not me, not my outriders, and no one on this train! The people of this wagon train and *I* signed a contract. No secrets, no information withheld from anyone, no matter the age, male or female, now… stand down."

Donna Jade stepped forward. "Lieutenant," She addressed him gently. "As you know, I am General Jade's wife, and you sir are out of line… Do you have any official paperwork to take charge and responsibility away from this man?" She pointed to

Charles, "If you do, then present them, and repay every person under his care for their fare."

The Lieutenant was speechless but knew he was in the wrong and silently stepped aside.

"Now that all my folk are ready for this meeting Sir," Charles's tone was back to normal. "Make sure that those you need to be present have arrived."

"Ten pots of coffee are ready folks, anyone who wants some is welcome to it." A lady from the train had called out. "Even you Soldier men, help yourselves."

"Okay Neal," Charles stated. "Tell us about your exchange with the Indians."

"The man I spoke with was Kiowa, he told me they had moved their village south. The Cheyenne has many tribes west of here and to the north. They have caused many villages to move south, according to the hunter I spoke to. They had also said that between here and Fort Dodge was still quiet. They said to avoid going to the northwest for a few days. There were many of the Cheyenne who had been running off to the nearby villages, killing the men of the tribe if they wouldn't join them and leaving the women to fend for themselves. Stating to us that the safest path for us to take is to stay straight on this trail and not venture north. That they meant for all of us to keep a watchful eye to the north." Neal finished with a calm but serious tone.

"What did the two of you exchange?" The Lieutenant asked his attitude seemingly a lot cooler now.

"He gave me a wolf's tooth, a symbol for a prayer, and safe travel," Neal replied. "I gave him a claw from the cougar I killed… It's a symbol of prayer for strength for his people."

The Lieutenant looks into the distance a bit sheepishly as he explains. "I ask all of you to forgive me for my outburst…"

The Lieutenant said with a slightly defeated tone. "It seems that I was out of line, and I truly am sorry for that." He tipped his hat to Mrs. Jade apologetically.

"Does this mean there will be any changes for us?" Someone from the crowd asked Charles.

"No, Jim," Charles answered. "General Jade sent us the same information when we were camped south of Wichita on the Walnut. However, it does tell me that the General's information was good and it was true," Charles smiled. "If no one else has any questions… we will be dismissed."

"Lieutenant." Mrs. Jade called out. "May I have a moment of your time?" The Lieutenant joined Lori's mom as they walked outside of the wagon train.

Lori was standing, embraced in Neal's arms. "Neal." She nudged him and pointed to her mother, "Watch this." They watched Mrs. Jade and the Lieutenant walk out into the tall grass. They had been conversing, and the four guards were spread out, a short distance from one another. Keeping their eyes on her at all times. Lori giggled at this sight commenting. "Poor mom."

"Yes… Babe, but she rescued you from that." And with that, they both chuckled and giggled to themselves.

The next two days were about the same. The traveling weather was good, as well as the trail was easily traversed. The evening camps would bring them to the western banks of the South Fork River. Firewood was plentiful near the river, so the wagons would collect extra when given the opportunity.

Before they reached camp, Neal noticed the light wind had come to a stop. The tall grass wasn't moving. "Look out at the grass Lori." He spoke with some intention behind his words. "Can you see how it isn't moving, how there doesn't seem to even be a whisper of a breeze?"

"This usually means that you are teaching me something, Neal." She smiled. "What am I looking for?"

"The temperature is going to change." He told her. "Not sure how soon, but the wind will come from the north, I think. It's November so winter is close. That's why I think it will be out of the North. Then add that there are no birds in the sky, and the wind will be strong. If you watch for these signs, you can be prepared."

"I can teach these things to my classes, Neal." She spoke. "What can I teach you?"

"You could help me with my schooling, once we get settled in of course." He told her. "I had finished the fourth grade before I was lost in the flood."

"I would love to Neal." Lori smiled. "You may not have used a lot of what you learned as a young boy, but it is still in there."

"Camps just ahead," Dusty stated as he rode up to them. "Charles wants everyone to circle up again, see you, kids, at the campfire."

"Tomorrow night we'll be at Kiowa Wells," Lori said. "Isn't that what Charles had said?"

"Yes..." Neal thought about it. "I think we are three, maybe four days from the Fort, Is that right Lori?"

"I think he said Kiowa Wells, Little River, then Fort Dodge..." Lori was deep in thought. "Tonight, then... yes three more camps, counting tonight, Neal." Lori was bubbling with excitement; you could see it almost radiating from her.

Lori giggled. "My bottom is numb; I'm going to have to rub it and squeeze it to see if I can get the feeling back into it. It will feel so nice to be off this wagon seat"

Neal growled. "Girl... you're killing me." He laughed. "You know, I could do that for you."

Lori had giggled. "I was hoping you'd say that." She was laughing as they circled their wagons into the big camp.

Kenny rode up. "When the two of you get settled in, I'd like to talk for a bit." Then as quickly as he came, he rode away.

When the camp had their meal and the folks got ready for sleep, Kenny brought Mrs. Jade, her father, and Dusty to the campfire where he found Neal and Lori waiting for him. With Mrs. Jade's four guardsmen in tow.

Kenny began with. "Linda is staying with Mom until I return. Our ranch and the Jade ranch is a few miles this side of the Fort." Kenny rubbed his face with both hands. "Now Mrs. Jade" He turned to her. "You and Lori left before Lucas acquired this land. Plus, your daughter is now married to my brother, who my folks think is dead. You two need to meet my folks because my dad and Lucas are partners." Kenny is pacing at this point. "Dusty is coming to my house because he is Linda's dad. We want him there for the wedding." Kenny Laughed. "I may need a pencil and paper to keep this sorted out." Everyone laughed. Mrs. Jade started to speak but Kenny cut her off. "Hold up Mrs. Jade" Kenny smiled. "So, if we all peel off the train at my house, then the only one we will be short… is the general. So… How can we get the general back there, so none of us have to backtrack… so to speak. I think I've said all I am going to." Kenny turned back to Mrs. Jade. "Got any ideas?"

Lori's mother stood up. "I'll write my husband a letter and tell him to come to the Morgans to meet us, send it with the Sargent." She smiled at Kenny. "Young man… you must have the jitters. It happens when young folks have too much time to prepare for their wedding day. You have thought it out well… I am proud of you!" she stated smiling.

Mrs. Jade hugged Lori, then Neal. The group enjoyed their meal and mingled with the individuals who were still around the wagon train. Once the sun had fully set most of the exhausted travelers had settled in the wagons to prepare for the next day and rested for the night.

By the time the sun had risen, the cold north wind had followed suit. Folks bundled in coats and scarves. The campfires were small, and crowded with coffee pots. With over a hundred people traveling Lori had felt as if everything was going smoothly and according to plan. She was enjoying the young Irish lady's chatter as the men were doing their part and the women seemed ready to move. "Do you have an extra canteen, Miss Lori?" Lori nodded. "Then fetch it for me now, we'll be fixin' yee man a refreshin' surprise for later."

The wagons rolled out and Lori had an extra wool blanket for them on the wagon seat. 'Pup' was on one side of her, and Neal was on the other.

"I'm glad that 'Pup' had decided he liked the wagon," Neal told her. "His age is showing a lot lately."

"You were right about the cold moving in on us Neal," Lori said. "The sky is clear so maybe it'll warm up some today." As they discussed the weather Kenny rode up beside them.

"Climb on," Lori told Kenny. "Me and 'Pup' are going in the back for a while." It didn't take much for Lori to coax the dog into the back of the wagon, Kenny was joining Neal now on the front of the wagon.

As the brothers talked, Lori filled two cups of hot coffee. The Irish woman told Lori how to wrap the canteens in blankets to keep them hot for a while. The cups were just past halfway so that they could drink them rather than wear it. "I thought you might like this," she said as she handed them each a cup.

"Now, where did you find this woman?" Kenny laughed.

Lori was standing on the floor of the wagon with the front flap on her back. She was leaning on the seat back and quite comfortably at that since she had been sitting so long already on that wagon seat.

"Neal has been turning things over and over in his head." She spoke to both brothers. "About how to, let's say introduce himself to your mom." Lori sipped her coffee. "Kenny has been worried so to speak about how the shock of this will affect her." She paused. "I think, I've thought up a plan to help the both of you with this."

"Please…" Kenny said. "I wanna hear it."

Lori began. "Neal carries a necklace, he showed it to me, each item, a token on this necklace represents the stages in his life. A bead earned for his first fish, one for his first kill, his first hunt, and earning his rights as a hunter, also one for his mother, and things like that. Each token is earned as he grows into a man. When he marries… this necklace is given to his mother. It's a story of his life until then. If you will learn this story, Kenny, you could set your mom down and tell it to her. Then tell her it's Neal's gift to her. She would realize its meaning and Neal could come in. Less shock. What do the two of you think of this?"

"That sounds good Lori…" Kenny told her. "Except you should be the one to tell her."

"I agree" Neal stated.

"Why me?" Lori asked looking confused.

"Because sweet girl," Kenny said. "The necklace passes to the mom when her son marries… and I think you can tell it better… and because I get choked up just thinking about this reunion."

"Kenny's right babe," Neal told her. "Besides that, … It would make me very proud."

Lori divided the rest of the coffee with Neal and Kenny, then she took a nap in the back of the wagon with 'Pup'. She fell asleep as the two of them conversed.

Several hours later, Lori drank water from Neal's canteen as the wagons rolled along. Neal put his arm around his wife. "Lori, are you warm enough babe?" He asked her in a comforting tone.

"I am Neal," She answered. "A nap was what I needed. It's been a good trip, with no deaths, no injuries, no big wagon problems. Everything has been good." Lori snuggled into his hug. "Us" she finished.

The camp at Kiowa Wells was cold. Charles ordered no campfires as the north winds were steady but not too harsh. The livestock were watered and the canteens were filled. Most of the folks on the train stayed in their wagons because of the cold. The covers on the wagons were the only windbreak for most of them.

Kenny and Dusty joined Lori and Neal inside their wagon. A small lantern was lit and it sat on a box low to the floor near the back of the wagon. What heat the lamp let out kept most of the chill out of the air as the four of them visited.

Neal had made sure Mrs. Jade and her father had everything they needed for the night. Her Soldiers had cared for the horses.

When the sun came up that next morning the Soldiers had most of the teams hooked to all the wagons. The train rolled out. They had no campfires that morning because the cold north wind was fairly strong again.

By mid-afternoon, the wind had calmed itself and it seemed warmer because of it. The camp was made on a wide rocky river bottom. It was a narrow and shallow stream that flowed that day.

When the spring rain came through that area each year the Little River was prone to flooding and it had carved out the wide gravel bar on both sides. It made the perfect place to camp for each wagon train that came through it in the summer and fall.

Little River would be the last camp for the train. The campfires were ready and the folks were preparing food and coffee. "Ten soldiers riding in from the west." An announcement was made amongst them.

The Lieutenant, Charles, and a few other riders waited for them. A soldier handed the Lieutenant the papers he carried. He read them and then ordered the riders to join his other men.

"Are you going to share your news with me?" Charles asked him and then added. "Or are you going to stay quiet and spread fear to the unknowing on this train? Or maybe cause panic? Would this make you feel like a big man to remain silent?" You could hear the anger raising in Charles's voice

The Lieutenant thought about it, "Call a meeting," he said with a dull expression. "I'll read it."

"Glad to see you've grown some common-sense son," Charles said. "I see the man before me is no longer a young boy."

"Meeting in ten minutes!" Charles announced to everyone, to spread the word.

"Fort Dodge Calvary… Front and center in ten minutes. Spread the word…" The Lieutenant called out.

Over a hundred souls gathered for the last meeting of the trail that year. "We will start our meeting with the Lieutenant, when he is finished with his news, I will have a few words of my own…" Charles gestured to the man next to him and states. "Lieutenant."

"Men of Fort Dodge, folks from the train, General Jade has sent news; it is as follows."

"There has been a big uprising several days west of Fort Dodge, Near the Colorado boundary. Our areas are undisturbed by the Cheyenne. You will have your men double up their guards until you have arrived here at Fort Dodge. These are for precaution as there is no immediate danger. Signed, General Jade."

"Charles will have a few words for everyone," The Lieutenant said as he stepped to the side letting Charles take the lead.

"That is all good news for us Ladies and Gentlemen." Charles started. "It has been a good ride, no deaths or injuries. It has been an honor to guide all of you across the trail. When we leave in the morning a few wagons will peel off at the Morgan and Jade ranches. I want those wagons and their escorts to take the rear of the train. The rest of us will go on to Fort Dodge. Those leaving us, I bid you farewell and hope to see you soon. Outriders remain with me at the campfire. The rest of you folks are dismissed."

"I'm going to Mom and Grandpa's wagon," Lori told Neal. "I will meet you back here at the campfire shortly." Then she kissed her husband.

"Outriders," Charles called, seven men were present. "Let us all have a seat. Dan, would you hand them all their pay pouches? Neal, your goods have been deducted from your pay. Any of you who would like to be rehired as outriders come by the trading post at Fort Dodge and sign up. The pay will always be the same for each. I was proud to have each of you. Take care of yourselves and your families, and may God bless you all. Thank you, you all will be dismissed at the Fort, except Kenny and Neal. They will leave us at the Morgan & Jade Ranch Lane. Now then, I see the coffee is ready if you'd like to join me, the calvary will take full watch this evening."

"Neal, before you open your pay poke," Kenny said, "I'll tell you that Charles didn't take any pay from you for your supplies when you joined us," Kenny smiled. "He always tells the new guys that, so they will accept the stuff. You see our contracts state that his train will provide anything the outriders need at the expense of the train."

Neal didn't know what to say. "He has been good to work for, I can't say that," Neal finally said. "What about his wagon and team that Lori and I have been using?" He asked.

"He knows we'll bring it in when we go to the Fort," Kenny told him.

When the wagon train rolled out of the Little River camp that next morning, all the folks on it were glad to be reaching their destination around noon that same day. They had come together as strangers to each other and would remain friends for many years to come.

When the wagons reached the Morgan & Jade Ranch Lane, Charles was waiting on his horse for them. He said his goodbyes again and promised to see them soon.

CHAPTER 8

FINALLY HOME

The three wagons and sixteen people turned up the lane. Kenny, Neal, Lori, Mrs. Jade, Lori's grandpa, Dusty, and eight soldiers.

"Linda, Betty…" Roy Morgan called out. "Kenny's home, and your Pa's with Linda."

"Tell him I'm in the kitchen Roy," Betty said. "I have to finish this cake."

Kenny kept Linda, his Pa, and Dusty outside and to the back of Neal's wagon. "Dusty knows about this Pa," Kenny said.

"Linda…" he kissed her, "I need you and Pa to just stay here with me for a few minutes."

Roy could see two women and a tall Indian going into the house. "Who are these people, son? And what…"

Kenny cut him off. "Pa… look at me… listen to me. Neal is alive… He found me Pa." Roy's face turns pale. "It's Neal, his wife, who just so happens to be General Jade's daughter, and Mrs. Jade who just went into the house. Let us give them just a few minutes. The women are going to… sorta ease Mom into the information.

When Lori, her mother, and Neal entered the house, Betty called out. "I'm in here Kenny… I need to get a cake made."

Lori entered the kitchen. "Mrs. Morgan…" She said, Betty looked up.

"Oh… my I didn't realize we had company." Betty dusted her hands off on her apron.

"I am Lori, and this is my mother, Donna Jade," Lori told her. "The General is my father."

"I've been looking forward to meeting you two, please call me Betty." She told them. "You are probably tired of the…"

Lori politely cut her off. "Betty…" Lori said. "My mother and I want to tell you a story." Donna led Betty to a chair where Betty would sit with her back to the door.

"Well… Okay… then, let me get us some coffee." Betty said.

"I'll get it for us." Lori smiled as she fetched the coffee.

"Is everything okay ladies? Has something happened to my Kenny?" Betty started to get up, Donna put her hands on her shoulders.

"Yes." Donna smiled. "But it was a good something, he's fine, he'll be in a minute. I'd like to start the story." Still, she was smiling at Donna. Lori was pouring the coffee.

"When a young Indian boy grows up, he is given a necklace. The necklace begins with its first bead to represent his birth, as he grows and learns, he earns other tokens as his achievements; His first hunt, and even his education. When he earns his place at each stage of his life." Donna was telling Betty. Donna could tell by looking at betty, that there was confusion spreading across her face.

Lori set their cups in front of them and took the seat across from Betty at her table. She pulled out a necklace and showed her. Lori smiled and then continued her mother's story.

The ladies heard the rest of the people enter the house. They heard Roy say. "I'm so happy you are home."

Lori continued her story showing Betty the necklace, and the tokens it held. "When the Indian boy becomes a man, and he is chosen by a woman, and he marries, that Indian presents this necklace to his mother. It is then hers to keep." Lori's eyes teared up as she smiled into Betty's eyes. "Neal… wants to present you with this necklace of his life as your son." She finished.

"Neal…" Betty's words were a whisper. "My Neal…" Lori nodded and pointed to the door behind her. Slowly she turned around, Neal was filling the door of her kitchen, choking back his tears smiling.

"I am home Ma, I am found." He said wiping a tear from his face

Betty's tears mixed with her smile as they held each other. When she released her son, she put her hand on his face. "I knew in my heart you lived." She spoke. "I could still feel you in my heart, I missed you and longed for you, but my heart wouldn't let me grieve your death." She told Neal.

Lori handed Neal his necklace and he took her hand in his. "This is the gift of life you gave me Mom," he said. "So, you can show all… with pride, of my accomplishments." He placed the necklace over his mother's head.

"So, you have married someone, Son?" Betty asked.

"Mom, meet my wife Lori Morgan, and my mother-in-law Donna Jade," Neal said with a smile on his tear-streaked face

Donna took Betty's hand "Her Pa doesn't know yet." She laughed.

The next few hours the family all reunited and talked. They ate bread and ham. Neal's hair hung long and thick over his shoulders as he didn't have it tied back today. "Son" Roy chimed in. "Do you plan on keeping your hair long?" Neal, Kenny, and Lori laughed.

"Well, Pa…" Neal smiled remembering. "As I grew up in that village, I refused anyone to cut it. I was in many fights over it." Neal looked at his mom. "My mom was the last one to cut my hair, and I swore that she, and only she would be the one to cut it again. The women of the village honored me with this, because they were… the ones in charge so to speak, and had the power over the rules. But the men, they did take some… convincing." Everyone laughed.

Lori sat down in Neal's lap, as the room told stories and talked. Then all of a sudden there was a knock at the door. "I'll get it," Kenny said.

"Good afternoon, Roy, my wife sent…" General Jade had started to speak but then stopped after seeing his daughter.

"Lucas," Donna said lovingly as she stepped into her husband's arms. The General held her tight but kept his eyes on Neal. His daughter was still in Neal's lap.

Roy stood up. "Lucas," he said. Do you recall the story of my son who was swept away in the flood long ago?"

"Lucas, you need to sit down," His wife ordered him. "This is going to take a while."

"Ladies, we need to be in the kitchen," Betty told them. "We have a wedding cake to tend to." All the ladies left the room.

Grandpa, Kenny, Dusty, and Neal told the General about Neal joining the train and how everyone met.

The General was laughing by the time Grandpa had told him that Neal had wanted to wait for 'his' blessing, when Lori, her mother, and he had threatened him with a firing squad.

"I was outnumbered Sir," Neal told the General. "But… I wouldn't change a thing."

"Welcome to the family son." The General told him.

Linda and Kenny were married that evening. She moved into the house Kenny built for them on the ranch. Roy and Betty Morgan's life was fulfilled with their lost son returning with his wonderful wife.

Betty and General Jade left for Fort Dodge after the wedding. The General Retired in July and took up his share of the business arrangement with his daughter's father-in-law.

Neal and Lori stayed in Kenny's old room at the Morgan house. Until their house was built for the next summer. 'Pup' claimed the porch as his own, as they all continued to live a happy, and honest life.

Fort Dodge is still a landmark of the old Santa Fe Trail. For many years it has been used as a place for military veterans of Kansas. A place where visitors can catch a glimpse of the history of the old wild west, as they walk through what is now written history.

www.ingramcontent.com/pod-product-compliance
Lightning Source LLC
Chambersburg PA
CBHW070355310726
48977CB00002B/459